F O R

. . . .

F R O M

. . . .

FOCUS ON THE FAMILY.

HYMNS
— FOR A —
Kid's Heart

VOLUME ONE

Illustrations by Sergio Martinez

Bobbie Wolgemuth
Joni Eareckson Tada

CROSSWAY BOOKS · WHEATON, ILLINOIS · A DIVISION OF GOOD NEWS PUBLISHERS

Hymns for a Kid's Heart
Copyright © 2003 by Joni Eareckson Tada and Bobbie Wolgemuth
Published by Crossway Books
A division of Good News Publishers
1300 Crescent Street
Wheaton, Illinois 60187

Design: UDG|DesignWorks, Sisters, Oregon

First printing: 2003

Printed in Italy

ISBN 1-58134-505-4 Book and CD set (sold only as a set)

All music arrangements copyright © by Larry Hall Music

Unless otherwise indicated, all Scripture quotations are from The Holy Bible: English Standard Version, copyright © 2001 by Crossway Bibles, a division of Good News Publishers.
Used by permission. All rights reserved.

LIBRARY OF CONGRESS CATALOGING-IN-PUBLICATION DATA

Tada, Joni Eareckson.
Hymns for a kid's heart / Joni Eareckson Tada, Bobbie Wolgemuth.
p. cm.
Summary: Recounts the historical and devotional stories behind the words
of many familiar Christian hymns.
ISBN 1-58134-505-4 (hc : alk. paper)
1. Hymns--History and criticism--Juvenile literature. [1. Hymns.] I.
Wolgemuth, Bobbie. II. Title.
BV315.T33 2003
264'.23--dc21

                       2003002480

PBI	11	10	09	08	07	06	05	04	03				
14	13	12	11	10	9	8	7	6	5	4	3	2	1

SPECIAL THANKS TO:

Mr. John Duncan
of TVP Studios, Greenville, SC,
Executive Producer of the musical recording
for *Hymns for a Kid's Heart*.

Larry Hall, arranger

Mrs. Lynn Hodges, Children's Director

Singers:
Jane Carter
Rachel Donaldson
Grace Douglas
Caroline Eddleman
Caroline Fisher
Misha Goetz
Matt Guthrie
Abby Schrader
Emily Smith
Alex Taylor

We are deeply grateful for the gifts of these friends
and accomplished professionals.

The publisher's share of income from *Hymns for a Kid's Heart* compact disc is being
donated by Good News Publishers/Crossway Books to Joni and Friends, the worldwide
disability outreach of Joni Eareckson Tada. For more information about Joni and Friends,
please write to Joni and Friends, Post Office Box 3333, Agoura Hills, California 91301
or call 818-707-5664 or go to the website—www.joniandfriends.org

Table of Contents

Introduction

to Grown-ups Who Love Children

Most of us would say that our scrapbooks and photo albums are among our most prized possessions. These are filled with treasured memories of people we love. They're priceless. Irreplaceable. For us, in addition to the photographs we cherish, some of our best memories are wrapped in the unforgettable strains of music—hymns that we were taught by caring musical encouragers . . . people who loved us, held us, and sang to us.

On the late night shores of the Chesapeake Bay, a crackling fire sending sparks heavenward like fireflies and our arms squeezed around our knees to protect us from the chill, a hymn-loving daddy softly begins to sing. My sisters and I join in.

This is my Father's world, and to my listening ears,
All nature sings and 'round me rings, the music of the spheres.

I loved my daddy more than a little girl could express, but to think that my Heavenly Father sprinkled the dark sky with a countless panoply of stars filled me with wonder. The words helped me to love Him too.

From her Virginia farmhouse kitchen my grandma spontaneously dished up hymns along with coconut cake and red Jello. Then, after dinner, the spot next to her on the piano bench was mine. Her hands seemed to glide across the keys; her voice was strong and sure.

Take my life and let it be,
Consecrated, Lord, to thee.

That was what I wanted too. I wanted to love God like she loved Him. I wanted to grow up to be just like her. So I learned the words and sang along.

Today every time we sing a hymn, our voices are thumbing through our priceless musical scrapbooks. We hear our daddy's voice, and we feel our grandma's touch. We're surrounded by these people who mattered to us, people who invested in us, celebrated with us, and sang to us. Precious people who wait in heaven for us to join them.

When we've been there ten thousand years, bright shining as the sun,
We've no less days to sing God's praise than when we've first begun.

Like us, many years from now, the special child with whom you're sharing this book will look back. And what you are about to do together just may become one of those indelible, life-altering memories.

The lyrics of the hymns will give them hope . . .

Under the shadow of Thy throne Thy saints have dwelt secure;
Sufficient is Thine arm alone, and our defense is sure.

encourage them when they are in pain . . .

When through the deep waters I call you to go,
The rivers of sorrow shall not overflow.

and give them a perfect picture of a loving God who created them . . .

Only thou art holy; there is none beside thee
Perfect in pow'r, in love, and purity.

And even though you may be in heaven waiting for this little one to join you, they'll remember you. And like our memories of a faithful daddy and a tender grandma . . . or a mother, an aunt, a neighbor, a grandfather, or a Sunday school teacher . . . their hearts will be filled with deep gratitude.

Somewhere, somehow there's a little moment waiting for you to use to teach a child a hymn. This book and CD have been created to help you do just that. It may be in the car, while you chop vegetables, or while on the porch rocker or at a holiday table . . . everyday moments.

We want to share the bounty of a lifetime of hymn-singing with you and your little ones. The deep truths that have sustained us, cheered us, and tenderly tied us to those people we cherish are waiting to be poured into the hearts of the children whom you love.

So we invite you to join us on a journey through the stories and the musical poetry of the past . . . a journey deep into the heart of a child. There we'll all celebrate together.

Welcome to the adventure of making priceless memories.

Bobbie Wolgemuth   Joni Eareckson Tada
Orlando, Florida   *Agoura Hills, California*

Hymns About God

Holy, holy, holy! Lord God Almighty!
All Thy works shall praise Thy name in earth
and sky and sea.

The Boy Who Thanked God

REGINALD HEBER, 1783-1826

Two wonderful things about a young boy named Reginald Heber amazed everyone who knew him well. First, he just loved books. He was a very fortunate boy to be brought up in a well-to-do home in England with a large library. Reginald was surrounded by all kinds of books, but he especially loved stories, poetry, and the Bible. From the time he could read, he loved meeting new people and going places inside his books. When he went to school, he would tell stories in such a lively way that all the children would sit around him and listen with delight.

The other special thing about Reginald was his love for God. Even when he was just a boy, he understood things in the Bible and made up his mind to become truly wise. He studied diligently in school and received top honors. He read a lot about Jesus and wanted to be like Him. He read that Jesus grew and became wise, and that both God and people loved Him.

There was a contest at Reginald's school one year, and he wrote a poem that won the top prize. He knew that God had given him the ability to write. After the ceremony, Reginald decided to go back to his room to thank God. He forgot to tell his mother where he was going. She was very proud of him for getting the award and came to find him. When she opened the door to his room, there was Reginald on his knees telling God how thankful he was for the poem that had won first place. So you see, Reginald was turning out to be like Jesus. He talked to God all the time about everything. And Reginald had a grateful heart. No wonder everyone liked to be around him.

Reginald wrote "Holy, Holy, Holy!" and some call it "the world's greatest hymn." He always told his friends that any words used to address God should be excellent and pure. He wanted the best language possible to be used when anyone talked about God or to God. That's why he says "holy" three times in the first line. There really isn't a word perfect enough to describe God. So he used the words that the Bible says the angels sing when they worship God in heaven.

Just like the children who used to gather around young Reginald at school to hear his stories, we can picture ourselves gathered around the throne of God. And we can sing the words the angels sing as they take their golden crowns off and place them on the ground in front of Jesus, just like Reginald did when he took his award and knelt down to give it to Jesus.

Aren't you glad a boy named Reginald studied hard and decided to let God help him write poems? Today you can ask God to help you, and He will give you new ideas. Tell Him you want to be like Jesus. Tell Him you want to have a grateful heart. You're never too young to do that!

BOBBIE WOLGEMUTH

— 16 —

A Kaleidoscope of Color

Have you ever secretly wondered if heaven is boring? Will we get tired of praising God after a few hundred years? No way! Heaven is *not* boring. The seraphim[+]—the big angels that surround God's throne—show us why. The Bible says that the seraphim call out day and night, "Holy, holy, holy." You would think they would get tired of repeating that, but they don't. That's because God is so great and glorious that no one—not even the highest order of angels—can ever run out of reasons to praise Him. There's always something new to discover about God!

Think of a beautiful diamond ring and how it sparkles every time you look at it from a different angle. Or a kaleidoscope and how its shapes and colors keep changing and glittering as it turns. Understanding the beauty of God is a little like looking at a diamond or gazing into a kaleidoscope. The longer you look, the more beauty you see. I can picture the seraphim catching a glimpse of God from one angle and gasping, "Wow, God is awesome!" But then they see some other aspect of God and shout again, "Whoa, we had no idea You were *this* wonderful, God!" Again and again God keeps revealing new aspects of His beauty and His holiness and His love.

The seraphim never get tired of shouting, "Holy, holy, holy" because God never stops revealing great and wonderful things about Himself. It's impossible to ever grasp all of God's wonderful-ness. And *that's* why heaven will never be boring!

JONI EARECKSON TADA

+ All words marked in this way are defined in the " Do You Know What It Means?" section at the back of this book.

Holy, Holy, Holy!

Ho- ly, Ho- ly, Ho- ly! Lord God Al- might- y!

Ear- ly in the morn- ing our song shall rise to Thee.

Ho- ly, Ho- ly Ho- ly! Mer- ci- ful and might- y!

God in three per- sons, Bless- ed Trin- i- ty!

Reginald Heber, 1783-1826   John B. Dykes, 1861

2. Holy, holy, holy! All the saints adore Thee,
Casting down their golden crowns around the glassy sea;
Cherubim+ and seraphim+ falling down before Thee,
Who wert, and art, and evermore shall be.

3. Holy, holy, holy! Though the darkness hide Thee,
Though the eye of sinful man Thy glory may not see,
Only Thou art holy; there is none beside Thee
Perfect in pow'r, in love, and purity.

4. Holy, holy, holy! Lord God Almighty!
All Thy works shall praise Thy name in earth and sky and sea.
Holy, holy, holy! Merciful and mighty!
God in three Persons, blessed Trinity!+

A Verse for My Heart

And one called to another and said: "Holy, holy, holy is the LORD of hosts;
The whole earth is full of his glory!" —Isaiah 6:3

A Prayer from My Heart

O Lord, You are perfect and holy. Thank You for Jesus.
I want to be like Him. Help me to be wise today and to have a
grateful heart. I know that I'm not too young to hear Your voice.
And I won't forget to thank You when You send good ideas my way!
Amen.

The Brave Caroler

MARTIN LUTHER, 1483-1546

C an you imagine what it would be like to have people tell your mom and dad that they can't read the Bible to you? Wouldn't it be sad if they were taken to jail for teaching you the Lord's Prayer or stories in the Bible? I'm going to tell you about a terrible time when that really happened.

In the country of Germany long ago the people could not get the Bible in their own language. It was read to them in a language called Latin that they could not understand. Only a few church leaders could read Latin. They would tell the people what the Bible said, since the villagers couldn't read it for themselves. Sometimes the leaders were dishonest and told the townspeople they had to give money to the church so God would forgive their sins. But the Bible doesn't say that.

Only a few people owned their own Bibles in those days. But God wanted everyone to have a Bible and be able to read it in their own language. Then they would be able to understand it and obey Him. God had a plan.

A boy named Martin Luther had a beautiful voice and loved to sing. He was sad that people didn't have Bibles and that they didn't sing at church. Only the boys who knew Latin could be in the choir. Martin Luther was so filled with God's music that he couldn't help but sing all the time. He wanted his friends who spoke only German to be able to sing too. Martin used his beautiful voice to sing all around the town to anyone who would listen. He would sing at the windows of wealthy people. They donated money, which Martin gave to poor people. His friends soon joined him and walked through the neighborhoods, singing as they went. This helped spread the practice that we call "caroling." The next time you go Christmas caroling you can think about Martin Luther, the little boy who loved to sing.

As Martin Luther grew up, he continued to use his musical talents and carefully listened to God. God gave him a wonderful idea. Martin knew how to put the words of Latin into German so all the people could read the Bible and sing songs to God in their own language. Then God gave Martin the courage to print Bibles and hymnbooks. Luther told dads, moms, and children that they could read and sing God's words in their own homes anytime they wanted to, from their own Bibles and hymnbooks. He told them they didn't have to pay money for God's free gift of salvation.

This made some of the selfish people very angry. They wanted to punish the parents. They made a law saying that anyone caught with one of these Bibles or hymnbooks could be put in jail. Sometimes they knocked on the doors of homes where parents were reading the Bible or singing from the hymnbooks and took the books away and threw them into a big bonfire. Isn't that sad? What would you do if someone took your Bible away from you? What if they told you that you couldn't sing Christian songs?

I'll tell you what Martin Luther and all the other brave Christians did. They just printed more Bibles and hymnbooks. They told the people to trust God, read the Bibles, and sing hymns. Their ideas changed the church forever in a movement called the Reformation. One of the hymns Martin Luther wrote to encourage the believers was "A Mighty Fortress Is Our God."

Martin Luther and the bold Christians knew that God was more powerful than the greedy men who tried to hurt them and take away their hymnbooks and Bibles. Today you can read the Bible and sing hymns in your own language anytime you want to because they fought so bravely.

BOBBIE WOLGEMUTH

Singing for God

S ometimes victory over the devil is yours for a song. I'm thinking of the time King Jehoshaphat of Judah and his army were about to go into battle against the enemy. The enemy's troops were better trained and had better weapons. King Jehoshaphat was very nervous, and he turned to the Lord in prayer: "God, we don't know what to do. But our eyes are upon You."

Do you know how God answered? He told King Jehoshaphat to gather a great choir of singers and send them out ahead of the army. The choir didn't have spears or bows or arrows to use against the enemy. All they had were their voices and song sheets. So the choir marched into battle ahead of the king's army, and as they sang praises to God, the enemy became confused and began to turn on each other. Before you know it, the camp of the enemy was destroyed, leaving Jehoshaphat, his troops, and the choir standing there jumping up and down and praising God.

This is why the Bible tells us to sing. You and I are surrounded by invisible armies of the devil who are experts at battling against people who love God—believers like you and me. But don't worry. The devil runs and hides when he hears you sing praises to God. When you sing, "A mighty fortress is our God," you are telling the devil to scatter; your trust is in the Lord. You have the best weapon of all—wonderful hymns about God. And victory is *yours* for a song!

JONI EARECKSON TADA

A Mighty Fortress Is Our God

A might-y for-tress is our God, a bul-wark[+] nev-er fail-ing; our Help-er He a-mid the flood of mor-tal ills pre-vail-ing.[+] For still our an-cient foe[+] doth seek to work us woe; his craft and pow'r are great; and armed with cru-el hate, on earth is not his e-qual.

Martin Luther, 1483-1546

Martin Luther, 1529

— 24 —

2. Did we in our own strength confide, our striving would be losing;
   Were not the right man on our side, the man of God's own choosing.
   Dost ask who that may be? Christ Jesus, it is He, Lord Sabaoth His name,
   From age to age the same, and He must win the battle.

3. And though this world with devils filled, should threaten to undo us,
   We will not fear, for God hath willed His truth to triumph through us.
   The prince of darkness + grim, we tremble not for him;
   His rage we can endure, for lo! his doom is sure; one little word shall fell him.

4. That Word above all earthly pow'rs, no thanks to them, abideth;
   The Spirit and the gifts are ours through Him who with us sideth.
   Let goods and kindred go, this mortal life+ also;
   The body they may kill: God's truth abideth still; His kingdom is forever.

A Verse for My Heart

Be strong and courageous. Do not fear or be in dread of them, for it is the LORD your God who goes with you. He will not leave you or forsake you.
—Deuteronomy 31:6

A Prayer from My Heart

Mighty God, I am so glad that You are like a strong fort that keeps us safe from the Evil One. Thank You for the gift of music and for my voice. Thank You for the Bible. Today help me listen to Your plan. I need You to make me brave enough to say and do what is right. Amen.

Joy on the Outside and the Inside

MALTBIE BABCOCK, 1858-1901

Have you ever met someone who seems to stand out from the rest? A student in New York had an unusual name and unusual gifts. His name was Maltbie Davenport Babcock, and he was talented in almost everything he did. He was a star swimmer and a good baseball pitcher. He was always winning sports contests. You can see why he was admired by everyone.

But there was much more to Maltbie than strong muscles. He had confidence and always tried to do the right thing. Maltbie was very sensitive and caring toward his classmates. He was fun to be around and liked to laugh, but he didn't laugh at others. He was careful to notice if someone was hurt or being teased. He stood up for the younger boys if anyone tried to bully them. And he bravely spoke up and corrected anyone who was using wicked language. This made everyone like him even more, except, of course, the children who were using bad language.

Maltbie was also a young man who loved music. He enjoyed singing and was a leader of the boys' choir and the orchestra at school. There was something else that made Maltbie very happy. He noticed beauty in the world around him. Music filled his mind as he walked in the woods and listened to the birds. The sights and sounds filled his heart until it overflowed with joy. One day he wrote a song about the splendor that he saw and heard. The hymn he wrote was "This Is My Father's World."

Maltbie Babcock grew up to become a minister. He loved young people.

They admired him too, just as his schoolmates had when he was a boy. They wanted to hear what he had to say because Maltbie always spoke the truth about God and His Word.

The unusual boy with the unusual name spent his whole life sharing the joy of God. Maltbie knew that God had made the world and everything in it. Maltbie wanted everyone he met to enjoy all the beautiful things that God had made—the mountains, skies, forests, and especially the sea. It added to his own happiness that people could sing praises to God right along with the birds. Today you can listen and look for all the sounds and sights that show God's creativity. Your own voice is part of the beauty that God created. Just like Maltbie, the boy with the unusual name, you can spend your entire life sharing the outside and inside joy with others.

BOBBIE WOLGEMUTH

The God of Variety

I had the most amazing experience the other day. A friend held a pear up to my mouth and asked me to take a bite. But it wasn't any old pear. She had picked it up at the Exotic Fruit section in the supermarket, and it was very large, wrinkled, and almost the color of a peach. "This is a pear?" I asked. I took a bite. I had never tasted anything so sweet before. And it smelled almost like perfume. "Wow!" I said. "This tastes great!"

It was my first experience with a South Asian pear. My friend reminded me, "God made that. Isn't that neat?" It was more than neat. It was wonderful and amazing. God made South Asian pears to show us how He creates things with incredible variety. He doesn't make just one pear; He makes lots of different kinds of pears. He doesn't make one kind of flower; He makes thousands of kinds. There are so many fantastic shapes and sizes, tastes and colors, aromas and textures in God's big world. And He gives every single fruit and flower—not to mention a zillion other things—to remind us that He is Lord and Creator of all. He's so great and majestic! This world does not belong to the devil. This is my Father's world! And you can find a zillion reasons to praise Him. That's something to remember the next time you're in a supermarket and you go by the Exotic Fruit section.

JONI EARECKSON TADA

This Is My Father's World

Maltbie Babcock, 1858-1901

Franklin L. Sheppard, 1915

2. This is my Father's world, the birds their carols raise,
    The morning light, the lily white, declare their Maker's praise.
    This is my Father's world: He shines in all that's fair;
    In the rustling grass I hear Him pass, He speaks to me everywhere.

3. This is my Father's world, O let me ne'er forget
    That though the wrong seems oft so strong, God is the Ruler yet.
    This is my Father's world: the battle is not done;
    Jesus who died shall be satisfied, and earth and heav'n be one.

A Verse for My Heart

Make a joyful noise to the LORD, all the earth! Serve the LORD with gladness! Come into his presence with singing! —Psalm 100:1-2

Prayer from My Heart

Father in Heaven,
everywhere I look there is something beautiful that You have made.
I listen to the sounds You have created.
You have made all things to praise You. And that includes me.
Thank You for my voice. I want to sing and speak of Your majesty.
That's when I'm happiest on the outside and the inside. Amen.

Hymns of Truth from the Bible

Jesus, the name that charms our fears,

that bids our sorrows cease;

'Tis music in the sinner's ears,

'tis life and health and peace.

Singing with Your Mouth Full

CHARLES WESLEY, 1707-1788

O nce there was a gifted little boy in England who loved to sing. His name was Charles Wesley, and he had eighteen brothers and sisters. His mother, Susanna, taught all the children their school lessons at home. She would wake them up very early in the morning so they could sing Scripture verses from the Psalms before they ate breakfast. The children used the Bible as their school textbook and read poetry every day. Soon young Charles was writing poetry all the time—when he walked or rode on horseback or traveled in a stagecoach. He liked to sing the poems he wrote and often used them as his prayers.

Charles had a wonderful and warm experience with God when he was a college student. A group of his friends met together every week. They called their group "The Holy Club." He and his school buddies talked about the things they were learning in the Bible and prayed for each other. Soon all the boys in the club were going around town telling everyone that living for Jesus was exciting. Charles decided the best way to tell people about Jesus Christ was to sing the message. He wrote songs and poems that told everyone about God and His plan of salvation. Remember how his mother had taught him to read by using the Bible? Well, Charles decided to teach people about God by using Bible verses put to music. These songs—or hymns—were easy to learn, and everyone liked them.

Charles said that just mentioning Jesus' name made fears leave his mind. Look at verse 3.

Jesus, the name that charms our fears,
That bids our sorrows cease.

When you are sad or afraid, you can do the same thing Charles did. You can sing and remember what Jesus' name stands for.

Charles Wesley knew that God could help rich or poor people to understand the message of God's salvation. And it didn't matter if they were very young or old. All they needed was a song to hear the good news. He wrote over six thousand hymns. He wanted lots of voices to sing out the greatness of God.

How many voices do you think have sung this great praise poem? Add your voice today to the thousands of tongues that have praised our great Redeemer. When it is filled with praise, it is okay to sing with your mouth full!

BOBBIE WOLGEMUTH

From My Heart to You

A New Body Someday!

W hen I broke my neck many years ago and became paralyzed, I was very sad. The doctors told me I would never walk again. They said I would never be able to use my hands. They told me, "Joni, you'll have to live the rest of your life in a wheelchair." I cried and became very depressed.

But Christian friends kept coming to the hospital and reading the Bible to me. The words of Jesus were comforting, and I began to feel hopeful. One Bible passage helped a lot. It was 2 Corinthians 4:17-18: "For this slight momentary affliction is preparing for us an eternal weight of glory beyond all comparison, as we look not to the things that are seen but to the things that are unseen. For the things that are seen are transient, but the things that are unseen are eternal."

Oh, joy! I realized that our life on earth is not the only life that will be! My earthly body is only temporary; the Bible promises I'll have a new, eternal body someday. As I trust and obey God in my wheelchair, I am preparing myself for heaven, where I'll be joyful and happy forever with Jesus. In fact, the more I obey God here on earth, the more I will glorify him there in heaven.

That's why I always enjoy singing the last verse of "O for a Thousand Tongues." I keep thinking of all my friends who are blind and deaf who one day will receive their sight and hearing. And there's that wonderful last part in the last line, "leap, ye lame, for joy." That's me! One day I will leap up out of my wheelchair. I can't wait!

JONI EARECKSON TADA

O for a Thousand Tongues to Sing

O for a thous- sand tongues to sing my

great Re- deem -er's praise, the glo- ries of my

God and King, the tri- umphs of His grace.

Charles Wesley, 1707-1788   Carl G. Glaser, 1784-1829

2. My gracious Master and my God, assist me to proclaim,
    To spread through all the earth abroad the honors of Thy name.

3. Jesus, the name that charms our fears, that bids our sorrows cease;
   'Tis music in the sinner's ears, 'tis life and health and peace.

4. He breaks the pow'r of cancelled sin, He sets the pris'ner free;
   His blood can make the foulest clean, His blood availed for me.

5. He speaks and, list'ning to His voice, new life the dead receive;
   The mournful, broken hearts rejoice; the humble poor believe.

6. Hear Him, ye deaf;[+] His praise, ye dumb,[+] your loosen'd tongues employ;
   Ye blind,[+] behold your Savior come; and leap, ye lame,[+] for joy.

A Verse for My Heart

My mouth is filled with your praise,
and with your splendor all the day.
—Psalm 71:8

Prayer from My Heart

Father in Heaven,
if I had a thousand tongues they would all say,
"I love You, Jesus."
Today help me to listen to Your voice
and use my mouth to honor You. Amen.

The Collection That Made People Want to Sing

RIPPON'S SELECTION OF HYMNS, 1787

D o you have a special collection that you treasure? Like baseball cards or coins or rocks or charms for a bracelet or sea shells or dolls or stamps? Maybe your mom collects something like teapots or angels or cookbooks. Some dads collect golf balls, antique tools, or cars. Whether huge or tiny, it is fun to have a collection and always be on the lookout for something to add to it.

A young man in London, England, had a very special collection. His name was John Rippon, and he collected hymns. When he was in college, John decided to hunt for the very best hymns he could find and put them into a book. He searched and asked his friends to help him too. He knew that people needed strong and helpful words from the Bible. He had a great idea. "Why not teach people with music?" If he could get the people singing words from the Bible, he knew they could be bold and courageous for God.

John selected "How Firm a Foundation" for his hymn collection because it is filled with great truth. Some of the people who sang it were facing terrible trials. They were tired and discouraged. This hymn helped them to be brave. Whether out loud or silently in their heads, they could sing the words all day and remember that God would help them. The smallest children could sing, even if they couldn't read. John Rippon's collection was making a difference by helping people think about God's Word.

"How Firm a Foundation" became a favorite hymn in England. Soon people in America started singing it too. Presidents, military leaders, and soldiers sang it when they were afraid or in great danger. It gave them strength when they were at war. They knew that God would not forsake them.

The next time you are discouraged or afraid, you can sing a verse of this hymn and remember who gives you strength. You can memorize the words that were part of a collection that made people want to sing.

BOBBIE WOLGEMUTH

From My Heart to You

The Right Foundation

I was raised on a farm that had a big red barn surrounded by weeping willows. My father was very proud of the old barn, for it had stood for over a hundred years. The stones in the foundation had been gathered from the fields and along the stream, and each stone was very large and heavy. The foundation was thick and sank deep into the earth. It's a good thing the foundation was strong—it had to support a barn full of hay, feed, tractors, and farm equipment.

One night we were awakened by horses' whinnying and shouts from neighbors. The barn was on fire! The fire trucks arrived, but it was too late. The big, red barn and all the hay and machinery burned to the ground. All the animals were safe, but the next day I sadly watched my father sort through the smoking ruins, looking for bits and pieces of his favorite tools. Nothing was left. Then he walked up to the foundation and ran his hands over the stones, which were still warm. He took a hammer and tapped the foundation. Then he stepped back and announced it had survived the fire. It was strong enough to carry the weight of a new barn. The next day Daddy began building on that foundation.

I was so proud of my father. And I was proud of the foundation of that old barn. It reminded me that sometimes "fiery trials," as the Bible calls them, can come into our lives. Sometimes awful things happen, and it seems as though everything goes up in smoke. But thankfully, if we know Jesus Christ as our Savior, we have a strong foundation in our lives—much stronger than anything that supports a barn or a house. So keep trusting the Word of God and the Lord Jesus. God is a firm—a *very* firm—foundation that nothing can shake!

JONI EARECKSON TADA

How Firm a Foundation

How firm a foun-da-tion, you saints of the Lord, is laid for your faith in his ex-cel-lent Word! What more can He say than to you He has said, to you who for ref-uge to Je-sus have fled?

Rippon's selection of Hymns, 1787

Traditional American melody
J. Funk's *A Compilation of Genuine Church Music*, 1832

2. "Fear not, I am with you, O be not dismayed;
    For I am your God, and will still give you aid;
    I'll strengthen you, help you, and cause you to stand,
    Upheld by My righteous, omnipotent[+] hand.

3. "When through the deep waters I call you to go,
    The rivers of sorrow shall not overflow;
    For I will be with you, your troubles to bless,
    And sanctify+ to you your deepest distress.

4. "When through fiery trials your pathway shall lie,
    My grace, all-sufficient, shall be your supply;
    The flame shall not hurt you; I only design
    Your dross+ to consume+ and your gold to refine.+

5. "The soul that on Jesus has leaned for repose,+
    I will not, I will not desert to his foes:
    That soul, though all hell should endeavor to shake,
    I'll never, no never, no never forsake."

A Verse for My Heart

Fear not, for I am with you; be not dismayed,
for I am your God; I will strengthen you, I will help you,
I will uphold you with my righteous right hand. —Isaiah 41:10

Prayer from My Heart

Father in Heaven, thank You for the strong foundation of Your Word.
The Bible tells me that You will be my strength when I am weak and afraid.
Thank You for hymns that I can sing that give me courage. I want to
remember Your words and Your promise that You will be with me,
no matter where I am. Amen.

Amazing Grace!

The Voice That Made a Difference

I'm going to tell you about a boy in England who helped change the world. His name was John Newton. He loved to sit on his mother's lap and listen to her gentle voice reading the Bible. She held him close and told him about great men in the Bible who loved God and obeyed his voice.

You will be sad to hear what happened when John was only seven years old. His mother died, and he was sent to a boarding school with a very cruel headmaster. So unhappy was he that John begged to be with his father, the sea captain of a merchant ship. It was at age eleven that John began to travel with his father and the rugged, rough-talking sailors on long voyages in the Mediterranean Sea. They collected goods to bring back to England to sell.

John missed his mother and tried to remember what her voice sounded like. But there was much to learn about the sea, and now he had to act like a man. While learning to sail, the only voices he heard were those of the husky men aboard the ship.

When he was old enough, John became a ship captain himself. But the merchandise he decided to sell is almost too dreadful to speak about. Instead of the usual collection of ivory, gold, wood, and beeswax, John Newton sold *people*. I am sad to tell you that he received money in exchange for young men and women who were dragged away to be slaves.

His large ship would travel across the ocean where strong young Africans were captured with huge nets and locked up with chains. Since the Africans were a different color and couldn't speak English, the sailors thought they could treat them like animals. This was a terrible thing. Taken from their tribes and families, the young blacks were jammed into the bottom of John's ship for the long passage back to England. Then they were sold to be workers. John Newton made a lot of money every time he sold a new load of black slaves. He no longer remembered his mother's voice or cared about obeying God.

But God was about to change John Newton's heart. Something stirred John's heart and made him want to read the Bible again. He began to eagerly search the Bible for God's instructions. With every page he read, John started to see the disgrace of what he was doing to the slaves. Suddenly he wanted no more money. He only wanted to obey God's voice.

With a change in his heart, John gave up being a ship captain and studied to be a minister. He willingly told everyone that he had done terrible things, but that God had forgiven him. John Newton wrote the hymn "Amazing Grace!" because he was thankful for God's forgiveness and felt clean from his sins.

One of the men in John Newton's church helped make laws for the land of England. His name was William Wilberforce. When he heard John Newton's story, William knew that God didn't wanted people sold as slaves anymore. He and John prayed that God would end the cruel treatment of the Africans. God answered their prayers, and after many years of prayer and hard work a law was passed setting all slaves free.

John Newton's mother had started a change for the world by reading the Bible to the little boy on her lap. God used His Word to change people's hearts and the laws in many lands. God does wonderful things when people obey His Word. The next time you sit and read the Bible, listen carefully. You just may hear a voice in your heart telling you something that will change the world.

BOBBIE WOLGEMUTH

Getting What We Don't Deserve

The word *grace* is very interesting. We usually see it in the Bible next to words like *justice* and *mercy*. Do you know what these *three* words mean? Let me tell you a story that will help explain these wonderful words from the Bible.

My friend, Mr. Thomas, has a little boy named Luke. Luke knew that if he disobeyed his daddy, he would face three spanks on his backside and then be sent to his room. One time Luke took some money off the kitchen table without asking. When Mr. Thomas found out, he told Luke to lean over to receive his spanking. Even though Luke was sad to be punished, he knew he deserved it. Mr. Thomas said, "When you are disobedient, you receive a punishment. *That's* justice. Justice is getting what you deserve."

But then something odd happened. After Mr. Thomas gave Luke two spanks, he suddenly stopped. Luke looked surprised, and he said to his daddy, "Why did you stop? That was only two spanks, not three." Mr. Thomas smiled and said, "I know. And *that's* an example of mercy. But you still must go to your room."

Luke went to his room. But then another odd thing happened. His daddy called from downstairs, "Luke, get your coat. I want to take you for ice cream." Luke could hardly believe his ears. "Why?" Mr. Thomas leaned down and gave him a hug. "Daddy, I don't deserve a hug," Luke said. His father answered, "And you don't deserve ice cream either. And *that's* what grace is—receiving good things that we don't deserve."

This story helps to explain the justice, mercy, and grace of God. He gives us grace upon grace—good things upon good things—that we don't deserve. And *that's* pretty amazing!

JONI EARECKSON TADA

Amazing Grace!

John Newton, 1725-1807

Traditional American Melody

2. 'Twas grace that taught my heart to fear, and grace my fears relieved;
How precious did that grace appear the hour I first believed!

3.	Thro' many dangers, toils, and snares, I have already come;
'Tis grace has brought me safe thus far, and grace will lead me home.

4.	The Lord has promised good to me, His Word my hope secures;
He will my shield and portion be, as long as life endures.

5.	When we've been there ten thousand years, bright shining as the sun,
We've no less days to sing God's praise than when we've first begun.

A Verse for My Heart

But be doers of the word, and not hearers only.
—James 1:22

Prayer from My Heart

Father in Heaven, thank You for Your Word.
I want to hear Your instructions.
Please help me to obey Your voice, even if it seems impossible.
You are the God who answers prayer and changes the world.
What do You have to say to me today?
I want to be a part of Your incredible plan.
I'm listening! Amen.

Hymns About Christian Living

Goodness and mercy all my life
Shall surely follow me;
And in God's house forevermore
My dwelling place shall be.

The Little King Who Heard a Song

THE STORY OF THE FIRST PSALTER

THE FIRST PSALTER, 1549

SCOTTISH PSALTER, 1680

A boy named Edward became the new King of England when he was only nine years old. Can you imagine being a king when you are only nine years old? Well, God had a reason for little Edward to be on the throne.

Edward's teachers taught the young boy about Martin Luther and the ideas that were helping people to believe that salvation was a free gift from God. Edward thought that it was very important to pray, so he gave the people of his kingdom a prayer book in the English language. It was called the *Book of Common Prayer*, and a decree went throughout the land that people must use it.

But there was still no hymnbook for the people in the English language. It was fine to have the new prayer book, but they wanted to sing in English too.

A man who took care of the royal robes for young King Edward loved to sing praises to God. His name was Thomas Sternhold. When the king was eleven years old, he heard a beautiful song coming from Thomas Sternhold's room in the palace. Thomas was singing from the Psalms. He was praising God with his gentle voice as he played on the organ. Young King Edward loved the music and the words. He felt such peace as he listened. He asked Mr. Sternhold to sing more Psalms for him.

Because Edward was the king, he could make laws for all the land. The young king decided that the people should start singing these beautiful Psalms all the time. He made a decree that a book of Bible songs should be printed. He asked Thomas to write some more songs from the Psalms. Then he had the songs bound in a book to give to all the people.

Edward was twelve years old when the book was ready. It was called a Psalter. Besides taking care of all the king's robes, Thomas Sternhold had written a wonderful songbook for the people of England. The book had a special note in it for King Edward. The message on the dedication page said: "Albeit I cannot give Your Majesty great loaves or bring into the Lord's barn full handfulls . . . I am bold to present a few crumbs which I have picked from under my Lord's table."

Thomas knew he didn't have riches to give the king, but the songs were his gift. And King Edward was more pleased than if he had received a brilliant jewel or a golden cup. The First Psalter was a great treasure to him.

So you can see that it is God who puts people in the right place with the right message at just the right time. Did you know that God has put you in just the right place to give a gift to someone today?

You can bring peace and beauty into someone's life with gentle words. Your greatest treasure may be a song. Maybe someday you will even have a chance to sing it for a king!

BOBBIE WOLGEMUTH

In the Arms of the Shepherd

Shepherd—I love this special name for Jesus. And there's a special reason why. The hills of Judea near Bethlehem are dry and scrubby, and there are many caves where wild animals hide. During the lambing season when sheep give birth to their young, sometimes wild animals sneak up on the sheep to attack the newborn lambs. Little sheep have become injured that way. They also become injured trying to walk on the rocky, steep paths beyond Bethlehem. When the shepherd begins leading the flock to green pastures, the weak and injured little ones try hard to keep up with the rest, but they can't. They stand there, shivering and calling for help.

But don't feel bad for a lamb that's injured. The good shepherd sees he needs help. He stoops down, picks up the hurt lamb, and cradles him in his arms. The lamb feels safe and cozy in the arms of the shepherd. He doesn't have to worry about wild animals or walking the steep narrow paths. He doesn't even have to worry about being too small to keep up. The little lamb is well protected in the arms of the shepherd.

And *this* is why I love to sing of the Lord as my Shepherd. I know I'm weak—especially living in my wheelchair—and there are many times I feel fearful of the future. But I know that whenever I call for help, Jesus will hold me in His arms and carry me through whatever danger may lie ahead.

When you sing this song, picture yourself as a little lamb who needs help. Believe me, you'll feel safe and cozy before you even get to the last verse!

JONI EARECKSON TADA

The Lord's My Shepherd, I'll Not Want

The Lord's my Shep-herd, + I'll not want; He
makes me down to lie in pas- tures green; He
lead- eth me the qui- et wa- ters by.

The Scottich Psalter, 1650

Jessie Seymour Irvine, 1871

2. My soul He doth restore again;
   And me to walk doth make
   Within the paths of righteousness,
   E'en for His own name's sake.

3.   Yea, though I walk in death's dark vale,
      Yet will I fear no ill,
      For Thou art with me; and Thy rod[+]
      And staff[+] me comfort still.

4.   My table Thou hast furnished[+]
      In presence of my foes;
      My head Thou dost with oil anoint,
      And my cup overflows.

5.   Goodness and mercy all my life
      Shall surely follow me;
      And in God's house forevermore
      My dwelling place shall be.

A Verse for My Heart

Oh sing to the LORD a new song, for he has done marvelous things!
—Psalm 98:1

Prayer from My Heart

Father in Heaven, You make my heart sing.
When I sing Your praises, I feel Your love.
Today I want to bring Your spirit of peace and beauty into my world.
As I sing in my heart and with my voice,
let my life be an encouragement to someone You love. Amen.

A Victory March for Everyone

EDWARD PLUMPTRE, 1821-1891

A young man named Edward Plumptre was known for being one of the smartest fellows at his college. The most famous universities in England had bestowed honors on him for his high academic work. But his friends and professors also knew him for being filled with a vibrant spirit of delight. His faith was exciting and contagious to all his friends.

One of the places that Edward loved to visit was the grand Peterborough Cathedral in England. It took over 120 years to build the massive stone church with colorful stained-glass windows and majestic, high ceilings. Inside the magnificent cathedral men and boys, women and girls would sing in special musical festivals. Marching down the long aisle with a cross and banner held out in front of them, the choir would fill the whole cathedral with glorious music.

Edward was able to compose hymns for many of the special occasions in the land. There were festivals for the Queen of England, Thanksgiving celebrations, and charitable events that always included exciting, new music. It was Edward who was asked to write for a special choir celebration at the Peterborough Cathedral. The choir would include young people and adults from at least twelve of the surrounding towns. What a dream come true for the boy who had a triumphant spirit and loved the grand cathedral!

Edward Plumptre didn't disappoint those who were waiting for his anthem. The noble words and heroic music of "Rejoice, Ye Pure in Heart" filled the high-vaulted ceilings as the singers strolled down the aisle. Edward originally wrote ten verses for the long processional. There were so many singers and such a long aisle that it took nearly thirty minutes for them to walk from the back to the front.

Edward's music was so marvelous that people could almost hear choirs of angels applauding from the rafters high in the ceiling. Like brave soldiers marching triumphantly past each pillar, the singers lifted the spirits of the villagers with the sight and exhilarating sound. With the cross and banner held high in front of them, the singers marched with joy. Surrounded by the musical encouragement, all the people returned to their homes after the festival with new excitement about following God. Joy was in the hearts of all who attended.

When you sing this great anthem, you can have the same joy as the children had in that first triumphant march. Overhead, you may even think that you hear the angels applauding so loudly that the rafters shake and the stained-glass windows rattle with the glad celebration of your victory march.

BOBBIE WOLGEMUTH

A Heart of Joy

W hen I was a little girl, every Sunday morning our church choir marched up the center aisle, singing and carrying flags and banners. I watched the cross being lifted high, and my heart filled with excitement as everyone sang louder and happier.

Sometimes, though, my heart wasn't very happy. Maybe I had fought with my sister in the car on the way to church. Or maybe my plans for the afternoon were ruined by the rain outside. I wanted very much to sing and be joyful in church, but my heart wasn't in it. However, I wasn't about to let my unhappy heart rule the day, so I would pray, "Lord Jesus, I know I'm being selfish, and I know that's wrong. Would You please forgive me? Thank You!" And then I would focus on listening to the reading of God's Word or singing the hymns without allowing my mind to wander.

And you know what? I would feel better halfway through the worship service. Often, at the close of the service, the choir would march back down the aisle with their flags and banners, singing, "Rejoice, Ye Pure in Heart." My heart felt light and happy as I sang. I had learned that having a pure heart, free of selfishness and sin, is the only way to really rejoice in God.

The next time you discover that things aren't right between you and God, remember this wonderful hymn. Be pure in heart, and you can't help but rejoice!

JONI EARECKSON TADA

Rejoice, Ye Pure in Heart

Re- joice, ye pure in heart, re- joice, give thanks, and sing; your fes- tal ban- ner wave on high, the cross of Christ your King. Re- joice! Re- joice! Re- joice, give thanks, and sing.

Edward Plumptre, 1821-1891

Arthur H. Messiter, 1885

2. Bright youth and snow-crowned age, strong men and maidens meek,[+]
    Raise high your free, exulting song; God's wondrous praises speak.
    Rejoice, rejoice, rejoice, give thanks, and sing.

3. With all the angel choirs, with all the saints on earth,
    Pour out the strains of joy and bliss, true rapture,[+] noblest mirth![+]
    Rejoice, rejoice, rejoice, give thanks, and sing.

4. Yes, on through life's long path, still chanting[+] as ye go,
    From youth to age, by night and day, in gladness and in woe.
    Rejoice, rejoice, rejoice, give thanks, and sing.

5. Then on, ye pure in heart, rejoice, give thanks, and sing;
    Your glorious banner wave on high, the cross of Christ your King.
    Rejoice, rejoice, rejoice, give thanks, and sing.

A Verse for My Heart

The LORD is my banner.
—Exodus 17:14

A Prayer for My Heart

Father in Heaven,
You are my great leader in the march of life.
I think about the cross and the banner of Your love as I sing.
I am full of joy. Because You are a great God,
I have a reason to be happy, give thanks, and sing. Amen.

The Girl with a Treasure

FRANCES RIDLEY HAVERGAL, 1836-1878

What would you say is your greatest treasure? Do you have a toy or a piece of jewelry that you especially value? Let me tell you about a girl who had a wonderful treasure. It was a treasure inside her heart.

Long ago a talented young girl was born to a minister and his wife in England. They named her Frances Ridley Havergal, and she surprised everyone with her musical talent. From the time she was very small she could sing like a beautiful songbird. When Frances was only seven years old, she began to write verses. She studied piano and was so gifted that people started asking her to play and sing at concerts.

Besides being a brilliant musician, Frances was captivating and delight-ful. People loved to be around her. She had a special enchantment about her, and everyone found her irresistible. Can you imagine why she was so pleasant? I'm going to tell you her secret. Frances wrote down her formula for her pleasing personality in one of her journals.

It's really very simple. *She prayed for everyone around her.* Oh, it was not an out-loud prayer, and the people she prayed for never even knew she was asking God to bless them. They just felt it. There was something so grand about being around Frances—it was the love of Jesus being poured over them by this little girl. As she played with her friends or talked to adults, she was secretly asking God to work in their lives and give them special thoughts.

Once Frances went for a five-day visit to a house where there were ten people. She noticed that some of them were "not rejoicers," and some didn't even know about the love of Jesus. She decided to spend her vacation praying for each of the ten people in the house and watch what God would do to change their hearts. Do you know what happened? Frances wrote in her journal: "He gave me this prayer, *Lord, give me all in this house!* And he just *did.* Before I left the house, everyone had a blessing. The last night of my visit I was too happy to sleep."

Just imagine—everyone in the house was different because one little girl decided to pray. And God didn't forget to give Frances an extra-special gift too. For that very night when she was so happy she couldn't sleep, all the verses of the hymn "Take My Life, and Let It Be" rang in her head, and she wrote them down. This is the treasure God gave to her. And you and I can memorize this prayer and keep it in our hearts wherever we go.

Now you know a very special secret. The next time you are around people who are not "rejoicers," you can pull out this treasure from your heart. You can pray for them. It will be fun to see what blessing God sends to them. Maybe smiles will be on their faces when you leave instead of frowns. Then you'll be like Frances. And you may be so happy that you won't be able to sleep!

BOBBIE WOLGEMUTH

But I Can Sing!

No doubt about it, I love to sing. Ever since I was a little girl I've been harmonizin' and making melodies.

After the diving accident in which I became paralyzed, my parents worried that I had lost the use of my body. They begged a specialist to come to the hospital to examine me. The expert stood by my bedside, took a pin, and began poking my feet and ankles, trying to see what I could feel. He wanted to see if I had much hope for getting better. He slowly poked his way up my legs asking, "Can you feel this?" and I would shake my head no. "This?" and again I would say no. He reached my waist, then my chest, and *still* I couldn't feel anything. I panicked. I was desperate to show him that I *could* do *something*. So when I still couldn't feel a pinprick at my collarbone level, I blurted out, "I can't feel that, but . . . but I can sing! Wanna hear me? Really, I can!" I then burst into a hymn.

I've been singing ever since. There's not a lot that I can physically do. Because of my spinal-cord injury, I can't use my hands. That means I can't hold things, and I don't have very much strength in my arms. I can't walk or run. But I *can* sing, and that's why I love this special hymn, "Take My Life, and Let It Be." I may be in a wheelchair, but I can still do a whole lot of things for God. I can pray and be loyal and patient, considerate and generous. I can encourage others and be a good friend and a good wife to my husband. I can help other disabled people through my ministry called Joni and Friends. But most of all, I can sing praises to God.

I hope you'll learn this special hymn and sing it with me as a prayer to the Lord Jesus!

JONI EARECKSON TADA

Take My Life, and Let It Be

Take my life, and let it be con- se- crat- ed Lord, to thee. Take my mo- ments and my days; let them flow in cease- less praise, let them flow in cease- less praise.

Frances Ridley Havergal, 1836-1878

Henri A. César Malan,1827

2.   Take my hands, and let them move at the impulse of Thy love.
Take my feet, and let them be swift and beautiful for Thee,
Swift and beautiful for Thee.

3.   Take my voice, and let me sing, always, only, for my King.
Take my lips, and let them be filled with messages from Thee,
Filled with messages from Thee.

4. Take my silver and my gold; not a mite[+] would I withhold.
   Take my intellect, and use ev'ry pow'r as Thou shall choose,
   Ev'ry pow'r as Thou shall choose.

5. Take my will, and make it Thine; it shall be no longer mine.
   Take my heart, it is Thine own; it shall be Thy royal throne,
   It shall be Thy royal throne.

6. Take my love; my Lord, I pour at Thy feet its treasure-store.
   Take my self, and I will be ever, only, all for Thee,
   Ever, only, all for Thee.

A Verse for My Heart

Rejoice always, pray without ceasing, give thanks in all circumstances; for
this is the will of God in Christ Jesus for you.
—1 Thessalonians 5:16-18

Prayer from My Heart

Father in Heaven, thank You for the gift of prayer.
Whom do You want me to pray for today?
Is there someone who needs a smile or a kind word from me?
Thank You for changing bad thoughts into hopeful ones.
I want to rejoice always.
And I want You to change others' hearts so they can rejoice too.
Amen.

Hymns of Prayer for Our Country

O beautiful for patriot dream that sees beyond the years

Thine alabaster cities gleam undimmed by human tears!

America! America! God shed His grace on thee

And crown thy good with brotherhood from sea to shining sea!

The Girl with a Journal

KATHARINE LEE BATES, 1859-1929

Have you ever been on an exciting trip and couldn't wait to tell your friends about the wonderful adventure? Would you be able to describe the places you saw and how you felt about each one? You might try to use words that would help your friends picture an orange sunset or a sparkling ocean or a magnificent mountain. One of the most inspiring hymns about our country came from a schoolteacher who had just such an experience.

In the summer of 1893, Katharine Lee Bates set out from her New England town to travel across the country to teach summer school. She was an English teacher at Wellesley College in Massachusetts and was delighted with the opportunity to travel to Colorado.

Now I'm going to tell you why you should never go on a trip without a pen and a journal: You may see something so wonderful that you'll need to write a poem about it! That's what happened to Katharine Bates. One of the stops on her journey was Chicago, Illinois. It was a huge city, ready to grow. An architect had designed a white stone display of tall buildings, showing what the city could look like when finished. Thinking about how the white buildings would gleam in the sun, she grabbed her pen and wrote a verse for the patriotic hymn, "America the Beautiful."

When she rode on the train past the wheat fields of the Midwestern states, Katharine wrote in her journal, "My New England eyes delighted in the wind-waved gold of the vast wheat-fields." She must have been an excellent English teacher to have spun words into a picture like that!

Have you ever seen the sky turn purple when the sun is setting? When you sing this hymn, you will notice a colorful verse describing a sunset at Pike's Peak in Colorado. Katharine Bates was so touched by the sight from the top of the mountain that she turned this hymn into a prayer. She knew that a powerful God was the Creator of the majesty and beauty she saw. In this hymn she prayed for our land and the people in it. Katharine knew that only with God's help could Americans love each other and work together like brothers and sisters.

Are you ready to go on a colorful trip through our nation? When you sing this prayer for the people and the leaders in our country, you can pretend you are on an enchanted ride over America as you travel "from sea to shining sea." Have fun, and don't forget your journal!

BOBBIE WOLGEMUTH

From My Heart to You

A Great Place to Live

America is a beautiful country. There are parts of America where fields of golden grain stretch as far as the eye can see. America has big, high, snow-capped mountains where you can camp by crystal-clear lakes. Our country has beautiful beaches where you can play in the soft sand and splash in the ocean. Some of the biggest farms in the world are in America where farmers raise enough cattle and corn to feed hungry people everywhere. Many fishing villages dot the coastlines of America where the ocean is full of fish, whales, and lobsters. America has swamps where alligators live and deserts where coyotes roam. There are many thick forests in America where all sorts of animals live. Our land has awesome waterfalls and huge canyons, mighty rivers and the Great Lakes!

Yes, America is beautiful. But what is especially wonderful is the fact that America is a land where freedom rings. This is why many people from around the world came to America hundreds of years ago—and it's why many people still want to come. Our country is a land where people are free to follow their dreams. Most of all, ours is a land where people are free to worship God.

Our land is a very special and precious place to live. Would you please pray for our country and ask God to keep it safe? Ask Him to help people trust in Him and turn from their sinful ways. Ask God to help people in our nation read and obey the Bible. Let's keep America beautiful, let's keep it free—let's keep it close to the Lord.

JONI EARECKSON TADA

America, the Beautiful

O beau- ti- ful for spa- cious skies, for am-ber waves of grain, For pur- ple moun- tains maj- es- ty a- bove the fruit- ed plain! A- mer- i- ca! A- mer- i- ca! God shed His grace on thee, And crown thy good with broth- er- hood From sea to shin- ing sea!

Katharine Lee Bates, 1859-1929

Samuel A. Ward, 1882

2. O beautiful for pilgrim feet, whose stern, impassioned stress
    A thoroughfare for freedom beat across the wilderness!
    America! America! God mend thine every flaw,
    Confirm thy soul in self-control, thy liberty in law!

3. O beautiful for heroes proved in liberating strife,
    Who more than self their country loved, and mercy more than life!
    America! America! May God thy gold refine,[+]
    Till all success be nobleness, and ev'ry gain divine.

4. O beautiful for patriot dream that sees beyond the years
    Thine alabaster[+] cities gleam undimmed by human tears!
    America! America! God shed His grace[+] on thee,
    And crown thy good with brotherhood from sea to shining sea!

A Verse for My Heart

For you shall go out in joy and be led forth in peace;
the mountains and the hills before you shall break forth into singing.
—Isaiah 55:12

A Prayer for My Heart

Almighty God, Your name is majestic like the mountains that You created.
Thank You for a country that is so beautiful. Thank You for pilgrims who
worked hard for liberty and freedom. Today I pray for America and for all
the people who live in it, "from sea to shining sea." Amen.

The Boy Who Loved Poems

ISAAC WATTS, 1674-1748

Let me start by telling you that a four-year-old is not too young to memorize poetry. The boy who grew up to write one of the grandest hymns in all of England memorized many poems when he was very young. He learned Latin when he was only four so he could memorize poems in another language. He knew five different languages by the time he was thirteen years old. Isaac Watts was the boy who loved poems.

There was something very wonderful inside Isaac's young mind. He would play with words and talk by making rhymes all the time. Have you ever heard someone say, "You're a poet and don't know it"? Well, that's exactly what Isaac was like as a boy.

Once, during family prayer time, Isaac opened his eyes and saw a mouse run up a curtain tie to the fireplace mantel. He couldn't help himself from blurting out,

> *"A mouse for want of better stairs,*
> *Ran up a rope to say his prayers."*

His father scolded him for interrupting the devotional time and told him to please stop making so many rhymes. Thinking that he was going to get a spanking, poor little Isaac turned to his father and said,

> *"O father, do some pity take,*
> *And I will no more verses make."*

Perhaps by making his father smile at the poem, Isaac was spared the punishment.

One day after church, Isaac and his father were talking about the music in the service. Isaac said, "God is so exciting, but our music in church is so boring." His father told him, "If you don't like the hymns we sing at church, give us something better, young man!"

Even though Isaac was only fifteen years old, he decided to do just that. He knew the Bible very well and had memorized many verses from the Psalms. It was fun for Isaac to put the words of the Psalms into music for worship that could be sung with joy. When the people at church heard Isaac's hymns, they were delighted. He kept writing hymns for all occasions. One of the songs Isaac wrote was "Joy to the World," which you probably sing every Christmas.

People were so pleased with the hymns that Isaac wrote that they said he must have had angels telling him what to write. They pictured Isaac sitting at his writing table with the angels whispering songs in his ear.

The next time you sit down, listen! Maybe you'll hear the whisper of a song in *your* ear.

BOBBIE WOLGEMUTH

Asking for Help

I love being around children. Maybe that's because I sit in a wheelchair, which makes me eye-level with most boys and girls. I don't have to lean down to give a hug, and they don't have to reach up. Sitting in my chair, I'm about the same height as most children.

I love doing something else in my wheelchair. I enjoy asking for help. Boys and girls reach for books off a shelf for me. They wrap a scarf around my neck. A little boy can hold a Bible and turn its pages for me. A little girl can give me a sip of water. "Would you please pick up my pencil that fell on the floor?" I will ask. Kids always smile when I ask them for help. They are glad to be "my hands."

Learning how to depend on others teaches me how to depend on God for help too. When I'm afraid, I go to God for comfort. When I feel lonely, God is the one I turn to. If I'm stuck with a problem, I ask God for help. I know He smiles when I ask Him for anything, and He loves for me to depend on Him. For as long as I can remember, God has been my help through the years, always showing Himself to be reliable and trustworthy.

This is why I enjoy singing, "Our God, Our Help in Ages Past." God was a help to His people not only during long-ago and faraway times, but He is our help now. If you feel afraid or lonely, remember that God loves for you to depend on Him. He will give you peace and joy, strength and a happy heart. And don't forget . . . He smiles when you ask Him for help.

JONI EARECKSON TADA

Our God, Our Help in Ages Past

Isaac Watts, 1674-1748

Attr. to William Croft, 1678-1727

2. Under the shadow of Thy throne Thy saints have dwelt secure;
   Sufficient is Thine arm alone, and our defense is sure.

3. Before the hills in order stood, or earth received her frame,
   From everlasting Thou art God, to endless years the same.

4. A thousand ages in Thy sight are like an evening gone;
    Short as the watch that ends the night before the rising sun.

5. O God, our help in ages past, our hope for years to come;
    Be Thou our guard while life shall last, and our eternal home.

A Verse for My Heart

"See that you do not despise one of these little ones.
For I tell you that in heaven their angels always see
the face of my Father who is in heaven."
—Matthew 18:10

A Prayer from My Heart

Father in Heaven,
You are an exciting God. I can be full of joy because of You.
Thank You for whispering songs in my ear and into my heart.
I want to sing and be happy.
I may even be a poet and not know it!
Amen.

The Schoolboy Who Sang of the Sea

WILLIAM WHITING, 1825-1878

Have you noticed that several of the young people who grew up to write great hymns lived in the country of England? England had great ships in their harbors and great singers in their schools. The children took their music studies very seriously. It was a high honor to be chosen to sing in the school choir.

Special all-boy choirs were sometimes chosen to sing for the king or queen. The blend of the boys' voices was angelic. There were some solo parts that remained a surprise until the moment of the performance. Each of the boys would memorize all the music, not knowing who would be selected for the solo. Every boy was prepared. As the singers lined up to walk onto the stage, the director would point to the boy who would sing the solo. Can you imagine the excitement of singing for the royal family? The boys dreamed of the day they would be chosen for the solo by the choirmaster. The boys also dreamed of the sea when they weren't singing.

One schoolboy who loved both the sea and singing was William Whiting. Not far from his school was one of the great Navy ports where ships would come and go. He thought of the brave sailors who needed God to protect them when they were out on the dangerous sea. William wrote "Eternal Father, Strong to Save" as a poem for a student who was about to sail to America. Later it became a favorite hymn and was sung on the ships of the British Royal Navy.

This hymn has become known as "The Navy Hymn" in America. The midshipmen at the Naval Academy in Annapolis, Maryland, love to sing it. Just like the boys who were ready at a moment's notice to sing the choir parts, the men and women who serve our country in the armed forces are prepared to defend freedom at a moment's notice.

You can pray for the brave soldiers, sailors, and pilots by using the words of this hymn. Whether they are on land or at sea or in the air, they can know that they are in God's care.

BOBBIE WOLGEMUTH

From My Heart to You

Safe in the Storm

D o you know about the United States Naval Academy? It's a big university in Annapolis, Maryland, on the beautiful, blue Chesapeake Bay. Men and women go to the Naval Academy to learn how to be officers in the United States Navy. When they graduate, they are skilled enough to serve as captains on submarines or officers on aircraft carriers. These men and women of the United States Navy are very brave and courageous, and they cruise the oceans around the world, on the lookout for danger.

When I was a little girl, I visited the U.S. Naval Academy. I walked into the large chapel and in the middle, I saw a big marble memorial honoring John Paul Jones. He was a famous Naval hero in the Revolutionary War, in which our country gained its independence from England. At the front of the chapel stood a choir of lots of men in white uniforms. They were sailors-in-training, and they sang this beautiful hymn, "Eternal Father, Strong to Save" in honor of not only John Paul Jones, but so many others in the Navy who had served their country well. The men had deep, strong voices, and they sang the song slowly, solemnly, and with great reverence.

It made me feel so good to know that people in the United States Navy—whether average sailors or admirals—have a favorite hymn. They must know when they are out on the big, wide ocean in the middle of a terrible storm and far away from land that they have to depend on God. Thank you for remembering to pray for all of the wonderful men and women who serve not only in the Navy, but in the Air Force, Army, and Marines.

JONI EARECKSON TADA

Eternal Father, Strong to Save

William Whiting, 1825-1878

John B. Dykes, 1861

2. O Christ, whose voice the waters heard and hushed their raging at Thy Word,
   Who walked upon the foaming deep and calm amidst its rage did sleep:
   O hear us when we cry to Thee for those in peril[+] on the sea!

3. Most Holy Spirit, who did brood upon the chaos dark and rude,
   Who bid its angry tumult[+] cease, and gave, for wild confusion, peace;
   O hear us when we cry to Thee for those in peril on the sea!

4. O Trinity[+] of love and power, our brethren shield in danger's hour;
   From rock and tempest,[+] fire and foe, protect them wheresoe'er they go;
   Thus evermore shall rise to Thee glad hymns of praise from land and sea.

A Verse for My Heart

The eternal God is your dwelling place,
and underneath are the everlasting arms. —Deuteronomy 33:27

Prayer from My Heart

Father in Heaven,
You rule over the surging sea and the wildest weather.
You are in control of all that You have created.
Today please protect all those who are defending freedom around the world.
Please send Your calm and strength to them.
Help them to feel our love and Your strong arms around them as we pray.
Amen.

Do You Know What It Means?

Alabaster: A whitish marble-like material used to make statues or vases.

Amber: The color yellow with a brownish tint.

Blind: Not able to see.

Bulwark: In times of war, a fortified defense was set up to shield the soldiers from enemy attacks. When spears or flaming arrows were shot by the enemies, the soldiers could hide behind the bulwark for safety.

Chanting: To celebrate by singing.

Cherubim: Guardian spirit beings, the second order of angels, who surround God's throne in heaven.

Consecrated: Set apart for holiness: dedicated entirely or devoted to God.

Consume: To use up or destroy.

Deaf: Not able to hear.

Dross: The scum on the surface of metal; worthless stuff.

Dumb: Not able to speak.

Furnished: Providing all necessary items and foods for a meal.

Grace: God's love and kindness or favor given to undeserving people.

Lame: Not able to walk.

Maidens meek: Girls or young, unmarried women who are modest and gentle.

Mite: A small coin; a very small amount of money.

Mortal life: Earthly existence that ends when people die.

Mortal ills prevailing: Dangers that seem about to overpower us and maybe even threaten our life.

Noblest mirth: Splendid joy, magnificent merriment, dignified joy.

Omnipotent: Highest authority, most powerful, able to do anything.

Our ancient foe and the prince of darkness: Satan, the evil one who is God's enemy.

Peril: Great danger or risk.

Rapture: Great joy, love, and pleasure.

Refine: To make pure, to take away crudeness or coarseness, to make more elegant and polished.

Refuge: A place of shelter and safety from trouble.

Repose: Resting with calm trust; freedom from worry or troubles.

Rod: A stick the shepherd used to defend the flock against wild animals and to examine and count the sheep.

Sanctify: Set apart and make holy.

Seraphim: One of the highest orders of angels who surround the throne of God in heaven. In Isaiah 6:2 they are said to have three sets of wings—one to cover their faces, one to cover their feet, and one to fly with.

Shepherd: A person who herds and takes care of sheep. A leader.

Staff: A stick the shepherd used to guide and rescue the sheep, to draw them together, and to lift newborn lambs up to their mothers.

Tempest: A violent storm.

Tumult: Loud, angry weather.

Trinity: The three Persons who make up who God is: the Father, the Son (Jesus), and the Holy Spirit.

Wretch: A miserable or unhappy person.

My Personal Notes

My Personal Notes

My Personal Notes

Welcome to the Family!

Whether you received this book as a gift, borrowed it, or purchased it yourself, we're glad you read it. It's just one of the many helpful, insightful and encouraging resources produced by Focus on the Family.

In fact, that's what Focus on the Family is all about—providing inspiration, information and biblically based advice to people in all stages of life.

It began in 1977 with the vision of one man, Dr. James Dobson, a licensed psychologist and author of 18 best-selling books on marriage, parenting, and family. Alarmed by the societal, political, and economic pressures that were threatening the existence of the American family, Dr. Dobson founded Focus on the Family with one employee and a once-a-week radio broadcast aired on only 36 stations.

Now an international organization, the ministry is dedicated to preserving Judeo-Christian values and strengthening and encouraging families through the life-changing message of Jesus Christ. Focus ministries reach families worldwide through 10 separate radio broadcasts, two television news inserts, 13 publications, 18 Web sites, and a steady series of books and award-winning films and videos for people of all ages and interests.

• • •

For more information about the ministry, or if we can be of help to your family, simply write to Focus on the Family, Colorado Springs, CO 80995 or call 1-800-A-FAMILY (1-800-232-6459). Friends in Canada may write Focus on the Family, P.O. Box 9800, Stn. Terminal, Vancouver, B.C. V6B 4G3 or call 1-800-661-9800. Visit our Web site—www.family.org—to learn more about Focus on the Family or to find out if there is an associate office in your country.

We'd love to hear from you!